MY ADVENTURE

Rehaan Nazim

August, 2020

Dedicated to my family and friends

The discovery

It was a beautiful fall evening when I was playing with my friend Tommy in the backyard and discovered something. It was a broken egg shell and looked gigantic, "WOAH!", I said. The pieces of the egg shell were a light shade of red. There was also a trail of yellow gooey stuff that went past the backyard into the woods. I was creeped out by the woods, so I said, "Let's play in my house".

It was in the afternoon when I decided we should go to the woods and explore. I just felt like we should investigate. We went into the woods and found something interesting, it seemed like burnt grass.

I just stood there with a puzzled look on my face. I didn't know what to say. I just stared at it, but finally Tommy broke the silence by saying,

"How did this grass get burnt?". "I don't know", I said.

Tommy suggested we go to my house and talk about this. We both ran back. After we had a conversation Tommy said that, we should just forget about all that has happened. Well, the problem was I just couldn't do that, instead I said, "I am going to keep investigating this".

Investigation

The next day I went into the woods, but this time without Tommy. I didn't find anything, everything looked the same just like yesterday. I came back disappointed. To distract myself, I went to play outside until my mom said, "It's time to wind up for the day" and asked me to take a shower. "You look pink and tanned because of playing so much outside", my mom said.

After the shower, I had my favorite mac and cheese dinner and went to bed without reading. "Shhh, hope nobody finds out".

When I woke up in the morning, I heard birds singing and other weird noises. I wondered what they were. It sounded a little like dinosaurs. Then I started adding up the pieces in my mind

and a second later I knew what hatched

out of those eggs. I couldn't wait to

meet Tommy. He had gone to the

library.

Later that day I went to Tommy's

house and told him about what I

thought hatched out of those eggs.

"DRAGONS hatched out of those

eggs!", I said to Tommy. "That can't be

true, Dragons aren't real", he said to me.

It is the next day, "Hey Tommy, I found claw marks on the ground where the burnt grass was". Tommy was excited and said, "Can you please take me to the claw marks?". "Sure", I said.

We both walked to the woods and I showed him the marks. "Hmm, perhaps you were right because, no animal with claws can burn grass, so I

guess this leads to what you thought it

was, which was a DRAGON".

The Dragon

After I went home that day I started having second thoughts about investigating because, dragons are sometimes unfriendly and they might harm us.

However, part of me still wanted to explore because I was curious. The next day when I went investigating Tommy came with me and we saw the dragon. It was asleep beside a tree and woke up when we were just a few feet away.

The little dragon didn't look mean or angry, rather it looked scared. I walked over to the dragon and touched its scales, they felt warm. The dragon was about the size of a backpack. I looked down at my watch and realized that it was 1:30 PM, "We are late for lunch", I said to Tommy and we both ran back to our houses.

After I ate lunch I went to Tommy's house, so we could go back to the woods where we saw the dragon. When we got there we couldn't find the dragon. I was very unhappy. We had found the dragon but, after just about 15 minutes it was gone. We just went back home.

The next morning when I woke up I hoped we would have luck because I really wanted to find the dragon. I also hoped that no one had found out about the dragon. It should be kept as a secret because, if someone knew they might tell everyone in the community. That would be a big problem because, people might try to take the dragon away.

Big Problem

Exactly what I feared happened today. Someone was spying on us when we found the dragon and they told the mayor, they also had a picture, so it came on the newspaper. When I saw the newspaper that morning, I ran to the woods and saw almost everyone in town searching for the dragon.

I had to find the dragon before them. I searched for twenty minutes, but I didn't find the dragon or any traces of it. Right when I thought all hope was lost, I saw a red tail, I ran over to the tail and saw a dragon. It was ten-times the size of the small dragon that Tommy and I had seen the day before. It looked like it was very angry.

I started running as fast as I could until I saw a cave in the distance, I ran to it and dove inside. It was some type of a tunnel and was pretty long. When I finally reached the end, it was like walking into a different world. There were more dragons. "This is probably where those dragons that were in the woods came from, Oh My GOD!", I said to myself.

I ran to Tommy's house to tell him what I saw. I also took him to the place where all the dragons were. He was amazed by the by the other side of the tunnel. "People will never forget our names if we tell them what we found",

said Tommy. "We shouldn't tell

anybody because there are greedy

people who might take them and sell it

for money".

The Party

It was my birthday today, we had a party. There was cake and other fun stuff. At the end of the party I just sat on the couch and watched some TV. My stomach was full because of eating too much cake and then I went to sleep.

It was 9:00 AM in the morning when I woke up. I went downstairs and had a croissant for breakfast. Then I

went to the garage because my mom
had told me that there was a surprise
waiting for me. When I opened the
garage door I saw an electric scooter,
"WOW AWESOME!", I hollered. This
was exactly what I wished for. My
uncle had gifted this for me. I wanted
to take it for a spin, so I opened the
garage and started riding it around the
community.

Later that day, I went to Tommy's

house to show my new scooter and then

we were off to the tunnel to explore

further. When we started exploring I let

Tommy use my scooter. He had loads

of fun using my scooter.

In the dragon world there were

unfamiliar sounds, like the distant roars

of the dragons and the high-pitched

chirps of insects. We both were happily

playing around with no fear.

Sam

Today when we went to explore
the world of dragons we caught
someone spying on us. He told us his
name was Sam. I requested him to not
tell a soul about what he just saw,
"Ok", he said. I was relieved that he
didn't argue.

The next day when we set off to
play I rode my electric scooter to Sam's

house. I found him playing video games on his Nintendo Switch. I told him if he wants to come with me and Tommy to explore he can. He agreed right away and we all went inside the tunnel to the other world.

After we were done exploring we reviewed everything we had found, a strange fruit, a colorful rock, and we saw a bird nest with a robin's egg. I had a good time with them. I then walked back to my house and played board

games with my family for the rest of

the day.

Interesting Items

The next day, Tommy, Sam and I played together in the dragon world. We saw turquoise, red, and green dragons. They looked beautiful soaring high in the sky. We also looked around to see if we can find something interesting. We got really lucky because we found a blue pebble that looked exquisite.

I suggested we should keep

looking for interesting things, so that is

what we did. We didn't find much, the

only interesting things we found are

green wood and a rock shaped like a

pigeon.

Some dragons came close to us. I

was pretty sure that one of them was

the little one we saw in the woods. I

started having thoughts that we should

build a door for the tunnel, so we could

avoid people from distracting or hurting dragons and vice the versa.

When it became 7:00 PM, I went home to have dinner. I was starving from all the playing and exploring. After I ate my dinner and went to my room to sleep, I was thinking of discussing with my friends about building a door for the tunnel to separate humans and dragons world.

"Ah ha! this could be our next project",

I said to myself.

The Door

I woke up early in the morning the next day, had breakfast and chatted with my friends using my IPad. "Hi guys, I think we should build a door that separates the dragon and human world".

When I texted my friends, they said that, it was a great idea and Sam said that he was very good at building, so it was going to be an easy job and

we all did it together as a Fall Project.

20 years later...

My friends and I are proud that we built

the door because it has kept dragons

and humans safe for years!